The Mystery of Mammoth Cave

Steve Kistler

Cover art and illustrations by John Yakel

authorHOUSE®

AuthorHouse™
1663 Liberty Drive
Bloomington, IN 47403
www.authorhouse.com
Phone: 1-800-839-8640

First published by AuthorHouse   5/25/2011

ISBN: 978-1-4634-0096-5 (sc)
ISBN: 978-1-4634-0092-7 (e)

Printed in the United States of America

This book is printed on acid-free paper.

Acknowledgements:
I would like to thank Janet Kistler and Joy Lyons for their
invaluable suggestions and editing help

Chapter I

"James, for the tenth time, STOP TALKING," Ms. Wilson insisted.

James could tell that she was about to lose her cool by the exasperated flutter that was coming into her voice. He had about decided to settle down, when a new thought occurred to him. He leaned over to Alex, who was in the seat beside him. "Does that woman think I'm deaf? She's already told me to be quiet nine times! How long..."

"JAMES AND ALEX! You have just lost today's break! Not another word from either of you!"

Alex was stunned. "Ms. Wilson, I haven't said a word all period! Why do I have to lose break?"

Alex's friends joined in quickly.

"That's not fair."

"It's James's fault, Ms. Wilson"

"Ms. Wilson, I know we've been studying about the Nazis, but I never thought you would act like that."

Poor Ms. Wilson. She loved her sixth graders, but, with the end of the year approaching, she would be just as glad to see the final day arrive as they would. *Whatever happened,* she thought, *to students who would sit quietly and not blurt out whatever nonsense came into their heads?*

"All right, class. You all should know by now that we don't all start talking at once. James and Alex, I'll talk to you after class about this matter. In the meantime, I don't want to hear a single peep out of either of you. Is that clear?"

"Yes, ma'am," the boys chirped in unison.

Jerking Ms. Wilson's chain is too easy, thought James. *She's too nice, so I can just do whatever I want until she gets mad and then act like I'm sorry. I can't believe Alex didn't know better than to sit next to me today. I'll sure be glad next week when we get to travel to Kentucky. I think we have little league practice this evening. Won't Ms. Wilson be amazed when I pitch the opening game of the World Series for the Indians in a few years? I wonder what's for lunch today.*

"James, are you writing this assignment down with the rest of us?" Ms. Wilson's insistent voice jerked him back to reality. Quickly, he scribbled down the assignment on the board. From what he was writing, it looked like they were in math class. He had kind of lost track.

The bell rang and the students loaded their ratty-looking

binders and math books into their book bags. Free for the next five minutes, they began to chatter about lunch, favorite video games, TV shows, baseball practice, cute girls, and cute guys. As the room cleared out, Ms. Wilson put on her best poker face and stared hard at James and Alex.

"James Murphy, we have four days of school left this year. How many times have I had to tell you to be quiet since September?"

James would have guessed slightly over twenty-five thousand, but he suspected Ms. Wilson wasn't expecting him to really take a guess at the number. He stayed quiet and tried to look sorry.

"James, can you *please* cooperate for the last three days? All the students are getting spring fever, and if you aren't at least playing along, then others will start to act out, too. We've had a wonderful year together, and I'd like to finish it on a really positive note. Do you think you can help me do that?"

Playing along. Now there was an interesting phrase, thought James. *School, like life, is basically a game we have to learn. If you play by the rules, everything seems to work out OK. The amazing thing is, there are rules which are spoken out loud and rules which are unspoken. For instance, Ms. Wilson has already taken our break time away for this afternoon, but if she's too busy to watch us, then she'll have to let us have break so she can do whatever it is teachers go and do between classes.*

"Yes, Ms. Wilson."

"OK boys. Since it's such a beautiful day, I'm not going to keep you inside during break. But tomorrow, I want your undivided attention during the entire class. Are we clear on that?"

Bingo, thought James. *You called that one, you old game-player, you.*

"Yes, ma'am."

As he walked to Mr. Curtis's social studies class, James reflected on their upcoming week in the country. His aunt and uncle lived in the heart of Kentucky, "way out past the back forty" as they liked to tell anyone who asked. Aunt Courtney worked at Mammoth Cave National Park, so James and his parents could go on all the cave trips they wanted. It had been three years since they'd visited Kentucky, and James was eager to get back to the woods and the hills. How could somewhere just one state away be so different from....

A hard red rubber eraser bounced off James's head. As the eraser careened away in the crowded hall, he saw Tony ducking quickly into Mr. Curtis's room. Tony would deny he had anything to do with it, but James knew what he had to do next. Exact revenge. Not the kind of revenge he would have liked to inflict on Tony, because students were not allowed to use Chinese water torture to slowly drive other students insane at Fairdale Middle School. James would have to make do under the circumstances.

He casually entered the classroom, checking to see where Mr. Curtis was at the moment. Mr. Curtis was a huge football coach. He was a massive man, reported to be six-foot-seven, but to James he looked closer to ten feet tall. Nobody messed with Mr. Curtis. Nobody. Not even sixth graders.

Mr. Curtis was putting some notes on the board and listening to students explain why they hadn't done their homework.

"Mr. Curtis, my mother went to the hospital last night. I couldn't get my assignment done."

"Justin, I might be a little concerned if I didn't know your mother works as a nurse on the night shift. Nice try; looks like we'll be spending some quality time after school together."

"But there's only three days of school left!"

"That's right, so we'd better use what little time we have left together to the best of our ability."

"Mr. Curtis?" It was Tabatha. "My brother did an experiment to see if my dog would eat my homework if he put peanut butter on it. So he put peanut butter on my social studies paper and my dog ate it!"

Mr. Curtis burst out laughing with a loud, easy cackle. "Tabatha, did you really just tell me that your dog ate your homework? Sorry about your luck. Justin, looks like you'll have some company after school today."

As students were coming into the room and the teacher was bantering with a few kids up front, James was watching for his opportunity to take care of Tony. He had his hand in his pocket, wrapped around his weapon of choice. It was a long, thick rubber-band, which James had dubbed The Enforcer. It had come off a bundle of newspapers and was approximately

5

twenty inches around. This meant that he could really draw back and do some professional enforcing when he needed to. James loved The Enforcer. In fact, he wasn't as worried about getting caught snapping Tony as he was about losing his rubber band. It could be a long time before he came across another high quality weapon like that one.

As Tony settled into his desk, James took out a pencil and headed for the pencil sharpener on the wall near the door. Tony's desk was in the row closest to the wall, allowing James to pass right next to his desk without raising suspicion. He was already picturing a large red welt on Tony's ear which would serve a as reminder to him not to throw erasers in the hall. As he approached Tony from the rear, James casually slowed down just a little and stealthily got The Enforcer out of his pocket. One step behind Tony, he held it with his left hand and stretched the rubber monster back a full two feet with his right. Ready, set...

"Murphy!!" roared Mr. Curtis. "What in the Sam Hill do you think you're doing ? Get up here and give me twenty push-ups right now! And I'm not talking about those girlie push-ups you were doing yesterday."

James was stunned. He had been on the verge of exacting a fully justified revenge. How could Mr. Curtis possibly understand? If he let Tony get away with beaning him in the head with an eraser, then every kid in the school would want a piece of James Murphy. Of course, Mr. Curtis hadn't seen the eraser incident and didn't even know about it, but that seemed a minor point in the larger scheme of things. To make things worse, James had been positive that Mr. Curtis was occupied at the front of the room just when he and The Enforcer were about to take care of business.

Eighteen, nineteen, twenty. He grunted and got to his feet. Mr. Curtis was there in front of him with his hand outstretched as if he were waiting for something.

"What?"

"The rubber band, James."

Not the Enforcer! He had to think fast or his best defense against friends and foes alike would be gone for good. "Mr. Curtis, I was just pretending to draw back on Tony. I don't even have a rubber band."

"James, do you see this cell phone?" Without raising his voice even slightly, Mr. Curtis held up a bright blue phone with little footballs around the edge of the screen. "You can either hand over the rubber band, or I can give your Mom a call and discuss it with her." Sensing that there was no justice in the world, James silently handed over the rubber band to his teacher.

"Can I pick it up after school, Mr. Curtis?"

"Sure, James. As long as your mother or father comes in with you." Both Mr. Curtis and James knew that he would never see his beloved Enforcer again.

Well, you win some and you lose some, thought James. As

he walked back past the smugly grinning Tony, James gave the other boy his best "wait until you see what's in store for you" smile.

In his mind, he was already traveling to the back woods of Kentucky.

Chapter II

The end of school always reminded James of switching TV stations before a show was over. One day you had to sit still and try to pay attention, and the next you were free to go outside and scream your head off just because you felt like it. A week after Fairdale Middle School had let out, it was only a distant memory in James's mind. He'd even stopped raising his hand to ask his mom if he could use the bathroom.

The Murphy family had been packing everything they would need for their two-week vacation in Edmonson County, Kentucky. They would be staying in a small cottage which Aunt Courtney had located, right outside the national park. She described it as a quaint little place, not far from her own home. The cottage was furnished, which meant the family wouldn't have to take as many cooking and sleeping things with them.

James's mom loved to make checklists. She made them for shopping trips, school assignments, errands, and, of course, for family vacations. The morning of their drive to Kentucky, she made James read the list out loud, while she and his dad made sure everything was packed in their minivan.

"Your suitcase"

"Check."

"My suitcase"

"Check."

"Swimming gear and towels."

"Check." James's dad liked to treat this exercise like a pilot preparing for take-off. Everything on the list had to properly stowed away before the van could roll down the driveway.

"Food and snacks."

"Check"

"Dad's girlie magazines."

"JAMES!" Every once in a while he'd slip an extra item into the list to see if they were paying attention. "Sorry, I wasn't supposed to mention those, huh Dad?" Everyone knew his Dad didn't have any magazines, but it was fun to act like he was hiding something.

"Fishing gear and tackle box."

"Check."

"The big bag with bug spray, sunscreen, books, and Dad's girlie magazines."

"James, if you want to get out of here sometime today, I

suggest you quit the shenanigans." His Mom was using her best that-was-funny-the-first-time voice, trying to keep everyone in a good mood for their long drive.

Soon they were all packed up and ready to roll. James had an entire seat to himself, so he spread out with his small notebook, his iPod, and the book he was half-way through. *One great thing about summer,* he thought, *is that I can read what I want when I want.*

The Murphys always played the license plate game when they traveled. They listed all the different states' plates they saw on the other cars on the road. Naturally, they saw Ohio first, since that was their own state. James started a list on a fresh sheet of paper. He numbered each entry. He wrote: # 1. Ohio. Once, on a family trip to the Grand Canyon, they had listed forty-two states. That was the family record, and one they might never break. James had great memories of that vacation, especially when he thought about his dad's Nikon camera falling what seemed like forever down into the canyon. His dad had put the Nikon down on a small ledge, and a curious ground squirrel had nudged it ever so slightly with its front paws. James was clearly innocent, and therefore he was free to enjoy the whole incident without worrying that he would somehow be blamed for the camera's death spiral.

The family got on I-75 and headed south. Quickly, they called out the license plates they spotted. James was busy writing his list. # 2, Illinois. # 3, Tennessee. # 4, Michigan.

The road was a major artery between the upper Midwest and Florida, and there was plenty of traffic on this early June day. # 5, Kentucky! James felt a thrill as he wrote the name of their destination state. The home state of Henry Clay, Daniel Boone, and Abe Lincoln! James knew he was stretching it a little to include Daniel Boone, but the explorer had been instrumental in settling the area.

"Dad, what other famous Kentuckians are there besides Daniel Boone, Henry Clay, and Abe Lincoln?"

"I don't know about Boone being a Kentuckian, James. I'm impressed that you know about Henry Clay. He was certainly influential in the early history of our country. All right, here's a tough one for you and Mom. One of FDR's vice presidents was from Kentucky...any guesses?"

Silence. James and his mom were stumped.

"# 6. Louisiana!" James called out.

"Good spotting, James. The man's name was Alben Barkley. There's a lake named after him in the western part of the state."

"What about Stephen Bishop?" his mom offered. "We are going to Mammoth Cave, after all."

"I don't know if you'd consider him famous," Dad objected.

"He was world famous during his lifetime, but that was a long time ago. Most people today have never heard of him."

"I've added Georgia, Florida, and Indiana," James chimed

in. "We're up to nine already. So who was this guy Stephen Bishop?"

"He was a slave boy who was brought to live and work at Mammoth Cave as a teenager in the 1830's." said Mom. "Eventually he became famous all across America and over in Europe for his knowledge and skill at exploring the cave."

"They made slaves of *boys*? That's worse than I thought it was. Why did that make him so famous?"

"He was born into slavery, James. When slaves had babies, their little children were automatically slaves, too. What's worse, the owners could sell children away from their own parents. It was horrible." She stopped and reflected on how bad it had been for the slaves. Then she went on, "I don't know all the details about Stephen Bishop. I'm sure that Aunt Courtney and Uncle Richard will be able to fill you in on the whole story."

Soon the happy family crossed the Ohio River at Cincinnati. They were in Kentucky! James bagged six more states, including New York, Minnesota, Alabama, Pennsylvania, Mississippi, and North Carolina. *I wonder why North Carolina's plate says "First in Flight",* James thought. *Maybe they have an air force base there.* He was about to ask his parents when he looked out the left side of the car.

"Montana!" he hollered.

"Nice going," congratulated his dad. "Those western states can be hard to find."

"Don't worry. We'll find plenty of states right in the parking lot at the national park." Mom told them. "Probably about three more hours, and we'll be getting close."

"Then Dad can relax and read some good magazines," James added.

Dad put on his pretending-to-be-stern voice. "Don't push your luck, buddy."

"Well, if you're not in the mood to read, at least you can look at the pictures!"

The afternoon wore on, and James decided it was music time. He put in his earbuds and escaped into the world of Green Day.

Aunt Courtney was on the porch when they pulled in. She had just picked two big heads of lettuce from the small garden beside the house.

"Hi, y'all. It's wonderful to see you again." She hugged her sister, James's mom, and hugged James and his dad too.

"Courtney, your garden and lawn look beautiful," gushed Mom. "That lettuce is perfect!"

"I thought we'd better eat it before the rabbits decide it's theirs." Courtney grinned. "Richard's still at work, but he should be home in half an hour or so. "

James had an idea. "Aunt Courtney, can you take us in the cave tonight?"

"No, James," scolded his mother, "give Aunt Courtney a chance to catch her breath. The cave won't go anywhere before tomorrow."

"Actually, James, I'm off duty this evening, but there is a Star Chamber tour at 6:15, if your parents don't mind your going. Ranger Matthew is leading the trip; I'm sure he'll be glad to keep an eye on you. In fact, Ranger Matthew is a direct descendant of one of the early slave boys who were brought here in the 1830's. His family has guided here on and off for close to two hundred years now. But it's up to your mom and dad. I'll take you tomorrow if they'd rather."

James recalled his earlier conversation with his mom about Stephen Bishop, the slave boy. "Is Ranger Matthew related to Stephen Bishop?" he asked.

Courtney smiled. "I didn't know you were familiar with Stephen. That's great. No, Matthew's family was brought to this area very shortly after Stephen arrived. Ask him. He's always glad to share some history with visitors. As a matter of fact, Matthew's been researching Stephen's history at the cave, hoping to locate his lost treasure."

"*Lost treasure?*" Suddenly, James was giving his full attention to his aunt's words.

"I wouldn't get too excited about it," Courtney continued. "Stephen left a box in the cave which has never been located. He told his wife, Charlotte, that it could change the entire history of the cave and make Stephen a wealthy man. There are lots of guesses about its contents, but no one is even sure the box exists."

Mom and Dad had been chatting out of earshot while James and his aunt talked. Dad spoke up.

"James, it's OK with us if you want to stretch your legs on a tour. We've been sitting in the car all day."

"Thanks, guys!" James was excited. He was getting back in the cave on his first night in Kentucky. And he was sure as heck going to be keeping his eyes open for that box!

Chapter III

About two hours later, after a delicious supper of fried chicken, green beans, and garden salad, James, his mom, and Courtney hopped in the car. Dad and Uncle Richard were sitting on the porch, taking in the balmy Kentucky evening air.

"Are you sure you're up to a two hour cave tour?" Mom inquired. "You've had a long day already."

"I'm more than ready. I want to see that place again, and I really want to meet a man who is related to former slaves."

"James, don't you know that almost all black Americans are descended from slaves? That's why we sometimes use the term African Americans. Their ancestors were brought here in chains."

"Wow. I guess I never thought about it quite like that," James reflected. "Anyway, Matthew is a historian, isn't he?"

Courtney jumped in. "One of the best we've got. His family has kept the oral history of this place alive."

"I can't wait to meet him."

James didn't have to wait long. Five minutes later they came across Ranger Matthew, lighting lanterns in preparation for the evening cave tour.

"Ranger Matthew!" hollered Courtney. "I have a young caver who'd love to join your trip, if you don't mind. He's interested in history, too. Matthew, this is my nephew James Murphy; he and his folks are visiting from Ohio."

"That's great. That's just great. Welcome, son." James liked Ranger Matthew instantly. He was a friendly man who spoke with a quiet dignity. When he welcomed James, he acted as if he really meant that he was glad to have him along. Suddenly, James wished Mom and Courtney would leave.

"Mom, Dad's probably wondering where you are by now. I'll see you after the tour."

Courtney and Mom had a good chuckle, and Mom told James to behave himself.

Promptly at 6:15, Ranger Matthew greeted the assembled people outside the Visitors Center. James thought he looked amazingly cool in his uniform and his flat straw hat. While Matthew told everyone about the upcoming tour, James started daydreaming about being a park ranger himself. He could just hear himself saying "Be careful with those lanterns, folks. They do get hot."

After Matthew's introduction and safety talk, the group

headed down the hill, carrying the lanterns to the large natural cave entrance. James was dying to carry a light, but Matthew had said that kids couldn't carry them, so that was that. As they were walking, a girl about James's age fell into line with him.

"Where you from?" she asked.

"I'm from Ohio. You?"

"Nashville. Except I'm spending the summer here, on account of a little trouble at school."

"No fooling? What happened?"

"It's a long story. I'm Shanda, by the way. And don't even think about making any Shanda Panda jokes. I've heard them since I could walk."

"No problem. I'm James."

They neared the cave entrance, and two bats flew out, swirling and diving.

"I love the way those things fly," James remarked.

"I love seeing them in the cave, too," Shanda added. "They just flit by like shadows. Sometimes you're not even sure you've seen a bat."

James liked Shanda already. First, she just came up and started talking to him. And, just as great, here was a girl who didn't need to try to impress him with a bunch of big talk. He wished that he knew some girls this friendly at school.

As they entered the cave, a cool breeze met them. Walking down the low, darkened passage, James took a few minutes to get used to his surroundings. The wall and ceilings were solid rock. On the floor were paving stones; it felt like they were walking on a sidewalk inside the cave. Soon they were inside the Rotunda, the first large room inside Mammoth Cave. It was huge! James tried to picture himself throwing a ball or a rock all the way to the ceiling, but he doubted if he'd be able to throw anything that high. The room itself was larger than the gym at school. A *lot* larger.

Ranger Matthew was describing how a crew of several dozen slaves had mined the cave dirt for saltpeter during the war of 1812. He pointed out the mine boxes and the old wooden pipes made from hollowed out trees.

"Someone went to a lot of trouble to recreate this whole mine scene," James murmured to himself.

"Oh, this is no recreation," said Shanda quickly. "These are the original mine workings from the early 1800's. The cave air and the chemicals in the soil preserve anything that's left in here. In fact, there have been seven mummies found in this place in the past two hundred years."

James was astonished.

"Are you telling me that those logs are almost two hundred years old? How do you know so much about this place, anyway?"

"Matthew's my uncle. Who did you think I was staying with?"

"You get to spend the summer with Ranger Matthew? That's awesome. Who made the mummies? You're not going to tell me there were Egyptians in Kentucky, I hope."

"No, nothing like that. They weren't wrapped up like Egyptian mummies. They were just bodies of Native American

Indian people who died in the cave. Some were preserved for over two thousand years!"

James couldn't believe it. He'd only been inside Mammoth Cave for about ten minutes, and he'd already made a new friend and started finding out some really cool stuff.

They walked deeper into the cave. James was enjoying looking around the huge passage they were in. The ceiling in this section was still way above their heads. The lanterns gave off a wonderful soft glow, and it was easy to see the rocky walls.

He had another thought. "How many mammoths would you say died in here?" he asked Shanda.

"None at all," Shanda smiled. "It's called Mammoth Cave because of its huge size, not because of any prehistoric elephants. Their skeletons have been found near the Ohio River, though - not too far from here."

The tour progressed. Ranger Matthew would stop the group from time to time to share some history with them or to show them a famous feature, like the Giant's Coffin. James listened to his calm voice and pictured himself exploring the cave all the way back in the early 1800's. His mind wandered, but that was OK. Ms. Wilson was nowhere nearby to make him pay attention.

As they walked on, he asked Shanda again, "So what did you do to get in trouble at school?"

"It wasn't that big a deal, at first. It's just that my fat-head principal had to make a fuss over something that day. I was playing the dollar bill trick in the hall, and he fell for it."

"The dollar bill trick?"

"You don't know that trick? You tie a very thin thread to a dollar bill and put it on the floor. When someone comes along and bends over to pick it up, you jerk the dollar away. It's a riot. I hide inside a doorway to a classroom and fool people before school."

"So why was that a problem?"

"It shouldn't have been a problem at all. But when Mr. Fat Head leaned over to pick up the bill, I jerked the string, and he actually tripped and fell on the floor. Everyone in the hall started laughing at him." Shanda was chuckling with delight, remembering her principal's face as he sprawled on the floor in the hall.

"WOW! That's great. So what happened?"

"He took me into his office and gave me this big Final Warning. If I ever did anything like that again, he would kick me out of school. It wasn't my fault he fell for the quarter trick the very next day."

"You played *another* trick on him? Are you crazy?"

"Well, I wasn't trying to play it on him, exactly. It just worked out that way. Sometimes I superglue a quarter to the floor in the hall when I get bored. The janitors really hate that. Anyway, just my luck, here comes Fat Head himself, and leans over and says real loud 'Which one of you kids lost a quarter today?' Then he tried to pick it up with about fifty kids watching him. We all fell out laughing!"

"Did he know you did it?"

"He wouldn't have, but a bunch of my friends kind of gave

it away by slapping me on my back. We were laughing so hard we could hardly stand up!"

James found himself grinning from ear to ear. Why weren't Ohio girls ever this cool?

"Shanda, I have one more question for you."

"Shoot, anything."

"Have you ever heard of Stephen Bishop?"

Shanda stopped dead in her tracks and stared at him. Her face got a serious look on it, all traces of her good humor gone. James actually wondered if he'd said something wrong. As Shanda waited, the group moved forward in the cave, leaving them in the fading light.

Finally she said "James, Stephen Bishop was the greatest American that ever lived."

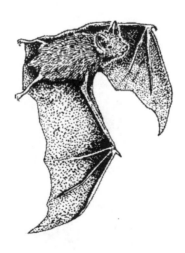

Chapter IV

The young pair had to hurry a little to catch up, spurred on by their trailing guide, Ranger Kasey.

Soon they reached the famous Star Chamber. They sat on benches between tall, narrow walls. When Matthew showed the group the ceiling of the room, the visitors gasped in wonder. At the top of the cavern, stars appeared to glow in the lantern light. James had to pinch himself to be sure he was still inside the cave. The minerals on the ceiling *really* looked like they were stars.

"Ladies and gentlemen, visitors to Mammoth Cave have been stopping in this very spot since the early 1800's," Matthew intoned. "Some famous Americans have sat here, including Ralph Waldo Emerson, in 1851."

James continued to gaze at the ceiling which gave the Star

Chamber its name, idly wondering if Emerson had ever been lost in the cave. The early slave guides might have played the first game of Where's Waldo!

Matthew told the assembled group how the illusion of sunset and sunrise in the cave had been part of the tour for well over a century. The idea, he explained, was for the guides to walk away from the group, taking all the lights with them. As he talked, the ranger and Shanda gathered up all the lanterns, taking three or four in each hand. Then they disappeared into a small passage in the nearby wall! As they walked further into the side passage, the walls reflected the fading lantern light in a twilight glow. Kasey encouraged everyone to admire the sunset illusion on the cave walls and ceiling. When the darkness was complete, she told them wonderful tales of young Indian boys exploring the cave thousands of years ago. As Shanda and Matthew returned, the pale rays of light again lit the walls and ceiling of the Star Chamber. Just before the lanterns reappeared, James and his fellow travelers could see the stars glowing brightly in the ceiling of the room. The illusion was complete; sunrise had come to the cave. The crowd cheered and clapped in appreciation of the wonderful display.

The group headed toward Gothic Avenue, and Shanda fell into line near James once more.

"Shanda, that was amazing. I really felt like the sun was going down inside Mammoth Cave." James could hardly believe all the amazing things going on during his very first evening in Kentucky.

"I love this place," Shanda replied. "I'd stay and live here if my mom would let me."

James summoned up his courage to ask: "So tell me, why was Stephen Bishop so amazing?"

Shanda responded, looking him straight in the eye. "Do you really want to know about Stephen, James?"

"Yes, I've been hearing about him a lot lately. Matthew mentioned him earlier in the trip, but I didn't really catch everything he said."

"It's hard to know where to begin. Stephen accomplished feats which would have been great anytime, but he did them while he was a slave. He single-handedly discovered about thirty miles of Mammoth Cave, which is still way more than anyone else has accomplished. He was the first to find Gorin's Dome, the Bottomless Pit, the Winding Way, Great Relief Hall, Mammoth Dome, the Rocky Mountains, and the Snowball Room. He was the first modern person to see the underground rivers and to find the eyeless fish which live there. He took visitors for boat rides, helped them open up new passages, and he saved a few people who were injured in the cave. Get the picture? The man was really amazing, James."

"Eyeless fish?" James was excited. "Are you kidding?!? How do they see anything?"

"James! Do you even think before you open your mouth and start talking?"

James was amazed. Shanda had repeated word for word the same question his sixth grade teacher, Ms. Wilson, had asked him just about every day for a whole year.

"Shanda, do you know Ms. Wilson?"

"JAMES! I can't believe you sometimes." Shanda exclaimed. "I'm sorry," she continued. "It's just that we were talking about Stephen Bishop one minute and you were asking me an unbelievably stupid question the next."

"My teacher says there's no such thing as a stupid question," blurted James. He wasn't irritated or hurt as much as he was confused. Shanda sure didn't seem to mind telling it to him straight.

"A question about how eyeless fish can see is a really stupid question. I'm sorry, James, but your teacher may have been wrong this one time." Shanda smiled. Even when she was criticizing him, he knew she didn't mean to hurt his feelings. "Come by Uncle Matthew's office tomorrow, and I'll tell you more about Stephen."

The trip was coming to a close. The visitors came up the stairs out of the cave and extinguished their lanterns. Ranger Matthew personally thanked them for coming while Kasey took care of putting the lanterns back in the metal shed. James didn't want to leave the rangers and his new friend, but he knew his mom and Aunt Courtney would be waiting in the parking lot.

"Thanks for letting me come!" he said as Matthew shook his hand.

"It was my pleasure, son," Matthew replied. "I'm glad Shanda had some company this evening."

"Uncle Matthew, can we show him Stephen's map tomorrow?" Shanda asked, hopefully.

"Of course, Panda bear, there's one hanging in the Visitors Center," her uncle answered.

"No, I mean the *real* map." James noticed she hadn't batted an eye when her uncle called her Panda, but he thought that maybe he shouldn't do that just yet.

Matthew smiled kindly at his niece.

"You know that map is a valuable piece of the past. It's not something we want to ruin by handling too much. However, I'll be in my office around ten, if you two would care to join me. Maybe we can take just a quick look."

"Thanks, Uncle Matthew!" Shanda gave him a bear hug around the waist. "James I'll see you tomorrow, if it's OK with your parents."

James found his mom right where she had left him.

"How was your cave trip?" she inquired.

James had no idea where to even begin answering that question. In one evening, he had made a new friend, met two park rangers, seen the Star Chamber, and heard about the famous Stephen Bishop and the lost treasure of Mammoth Cave. It was more excitement than he'd ever had in a whole week of school.

"Pretty good," he smiled.

Chapter V

James awoke the next day to a sweet Kentucky summer morning. It was only a little after seven o'clock, but the sunshine was bright and bird songs filled the air. A soft breeze came through his window. It promised to be a great day.

Coming into the living room, he saw Aunt Courtney in her park uniform, getting ready to leave.

"Good morning, James," she beamed. "Your mom told me you had a good time with Matthew and Shanda last night."

"It was awesome." James grinned back at her. "I'd forgotten how big that place is! Ranger Matthew was a great guide, too."

"Most of our guides here are exceptional. We're part of the living history of this area, and we all take great pride in that."

James wondered about the phrase, *living history*, and what it meant. He was going to ask Aunt Courtney, when his mother and father came in from the back yard.

"Oh, James, what a glorious morning!" his mom greeted him. "Dad and I were watching a pair of pileated woodpeckers feeding at the edge of the forest. What beautiful birds!"

James liked going on vacation for lots of reasons, but one of the main ones was the fun of watching his parents relax and enjoy themselves so much.

Dad spoke up, "What do you want to do today, James? We can hike or go canoeing if you like. And Aunt Courtney has kindly offered to take us on her lantern tour later today."

"Dad, I met some people who know a lot about Stephen Bishop last night. Do you think I might be able to visit Ranger Matthew and his niece Shanda a little later this morning? I would really like to try some canoeing too, some time."

"Well, we have a whole week stretching ahead of us. I think there should be time to do everything, don't you? Where are you supposed to meet them?"

"Matthew has an office in the Visitors Center. He said he'd be there about ten o'clock."

"I don't see why that should be any problem, James. How about some breakfast?"

After they had eaten, James and his parents started exploring the woods around their cabin. They soon came to a large rock face, kind of a cliff up against a hillside in the forest.

"What are these perfectly round holes in these big rocks?" James wondered aloud.

"Good find, James!" his father exclaimed. "Those are

grinding holes, places where American Indians used to grind corn into flour."

James was amazed. "Are you kidding me? There were Indians living right here where we are now?"

"It sure looks that way. They probably liked the shelter of this cliff and being close to that stream down there."

"Hey, boys, look at this!" Mom was excited about finding something nearby. When they had scrambled over to her, she showed them her find. In a small sandy spot at the base of the cliff, there was a pile of very thin rock pieces. They looked like flakes.

"What is it, Mom?" James asked.

"This is a knapping site, James. A place where the Native Americans used to shaped flint to make spear points and arrow heads."

"No way!" James exclaimed. "They made arrowheads right here? I wonder if any Indians are still lurking in the woods, guarding over this spot." Suddenly, James clutched his chest with both hands and made a horrible screeching noise.

"I've been hit by an arrow! Goodbye, Mom and Dad! You were pretty good parents." He dropped to his knees, gasping and flopping on the ground. Mom and Dad were laughing their heads off. James continued to roll around for several minutes, just to be sure his performance was complete.

"It doesn't take quite that long to die, cowboy," said his mom. "Try to get it down to five minutes next time."

"Let's hunt for arrowheads," Dad suggested. "I hear they're not too hard to find."

The three adventurers spent a happy hour exploring the old Indian site, turning up occasional pieces of flint and some charcoal. Dad found what might have been an arrowhead, but it was in poor condition and it was hard to really tell what it was.

Their morning explorations were cut short when Mom looked at her watch. "James, if you want to meet Matthew and Shanda, we'd better get going."

"Yes, let's." James was eager to talk to Shanda and Ranger Matthew and to see the famous Stephen Bishop map. He wondered if the map would yield any clues to Stephen's mysterious box.

Arriving at the Visitors Center, the family was surprised to see how crowded it was. There were three park rangers at the information desk, telling new arrivals about cave tours, camping, and lots of other things. James approached a young lady whose name tag read Violet.

"Hi, I'm looking for Ranger Matthew," he told her.

Violet smiled. James fleetingly wondered if everyone was this nice in Kentucky, or was it just the park people specifically. Everyone he had met so far seemed relaxed and friendly. "Matthew is back in our research room. Come on, I'll show you where he is."

Sure enough, Matthew and Shanda were in the private room. They were standing over a large table, with two oversized pictures on it. James noticed their family resemblance

34

immediately, wondering why it hadn't been obvious to him the night before. They looked up as James and his parents entered the room.

"Hi James." Shanda smiled. James felt happy to see his new friend again so soon.

"Hey," he said. "These are my parents. Mom, Dad, meet Shanda and Matthew. Ranger Matthew is her uncle."

They said their hellos and the adults shook hands. *I wonder why on earth people shake hands,* thought James. *Don't Eskimos rub noses or something?* He didn't get too long to think about it, as Matthew was showing his parents his workspace.

"We are encouraged to do research here at the park," he was saying. "There are many historical documents and articles in our files. It's fun to pick a project and pursue it for a year or two."

Wow, thought James, *a year or two! I've never found anything to keep me interested that long in school.*

As if he were a mind reader, Matthew added "It's not like an assignment, James. We research because we love the excitement of discovering history for ourselves. I've been studying everything I can find on Stephen Bishop since last spring. Shanda's been a huge help this summer." His niece smiled, pleased with Matthew's kind words.

"What have you discovered about Stephen so far, Mr. Matthew?" inquired James.

The ranger chuckled. "First of all, it's just Matthew. You don't need to "mister" me, unless of course I come to speak at your school someday. I'll be glad to share what I've learned with you, but I don't want to bore you all to tears."

James's mom spoke up. "Matthew, if you don't mind having James with you, we might go look around the Visitors Center a while. Would we be imposing too much to leave him with you?"

"Not at all. Panda Bear and I are glad for his company. It's not any imposition on us, I assure you."

"Wonderful" said Mom. "Should we explore a bit and come back in half an hour?"

Matthew turned to James. "How about it, James? Do you want to learn about Stephen first hand? Shanda and I were just about to go take some pictures of Turtle Rock."

James couldn't believe what he was hearing. His parents and Matthew were all agreeing to let him have some real fun with Matthew and Shanda. He had no idea what they were planning, but it sounded like the day could only get better. He really didn't know what to say first, but he finally asked, "Where's Turtle Rock?"

"It's in the cave, down a passage behind the Giant's Coffin. You remember that from last night, I guess. Ms. Murphy, do you mind if we keep him a little longer, say, until midafternoon? I'd be glad to run him home."

"It's OK with us if you can stand him that long," laughed Mom. "James, you are to be..."

"I know, Mom. Bestest behavior." He smiled. Some time earlier, James and his mom had settled on the phrase "bestest behavior," for times when he was getting a great opportunity of some sort and he better not mess it up.

"Great. You three have fun. Thanks, so much, Matthew. It's good to meet you, and you too, Shanda." And with that, James was alone with his two new friends. At last, he was going to find out the real secret behind the legend of Stephen Bishop!

Chapter VI

James, Matthew, and Shanda were walking through the huge cave passages by themselves. They each wore a helmet equipped with a headlight, and they each had a flashlight too.

The mammoth passages and rooms were even more amazing than James had remembered. Without the tour group and the constant chatter, a peaceful sense of silence embraced the ancient cave. While their head lamps were plenty bright enough, they only lit the regions directly in front of them. James could see lots of interesting rocks and shadows on either side, but he could only get a good look at them by turning his head and looking directly at them. It was an odd sensation.

As they walked, Matthew filled them in on his recent research. "Stephen Bishop accomplished many things in his young life. He was brought here as a slave when he was seventeen years old. He became such a successful guide and explorer that his owner brought more slaves to the cave to expand his business. There are many stories of his exploration and of his heroic acts. I'm not sure that they're all true, but I'm finding out some great information in our early records. He was very proud of his work in this cave, and he loved this place as much as anyone before or since."

"Was he ever set free?" James wondered out loud.

"Actually, yes. He was set free in 1856, but he died only a year later. He was only thirty-seven years old at the time."

"How did he die, Matthew? Was he killed?"

"Probably not. Documents from that era list an 'unknown disease' as a cause of death, but I doubt if he had much chance to get to a doctor when he became ill. It could have been anything from the flu to consumption."

James wondered what on earth consumption was. He'd never heard of anyone staying home from school because of consumption. Maybe it was a disease which people only caught in the old days.

"Matthew, Aunt Courtney said that Stephen left a treasure in the cave. Is that true?"

"We think it is, James, except no one has seen any sign of it in the last one hundred fifty years. Of course if it really is in the cave, it's probably in good condition. There's no wind or weather down here to make things erode or rust. We do know that Stephen told Charlotte that he had hidden a box in the cave and that the contents of the box would make them rich. It's a terrific mystery."

Shanda had been walking quietly with them, as her Uncle Matthew told James the story of the famous slave guide. Now she joined the conversation.

"What do you think the treasure was, Uncle Matthew?" she asked.

"No one really knows, Shanda. We can only guess from the few clues we have. It would have to be something which would fit into a small metal box."

"Gold," James murmured.

"Maybe." said Matthew, "But I'm not sure you could put enough gold into a small box to make you rich. Of course, having once been enslaved, Stephen and Charlotte might have a different notion of being rich than most folks."

"Uncle Matthew, you don't think Stephen or Charlotte stole something valuable like jewelry, do you?" Shanda was clearly worried. The last thing she wanted was to discover that her hero was a thief.

"We'll follow the evidence wherever it takes us, Shanda. But I wouldn't worry too much about the treasure being stolen... Stephen was known as an honest man."

The party had reached a trail that was wide and easy to walk through, but it was clearly not part of any tour route. The ceiling lowered down to ten or twelve feet over their heads, and the walls were maybe twenty feet apart.

"Cool passage!" James exclaimed. "Where are we, Matthew?"

"This trail is called Pensico Avenue. And here's Turtle Rock."

They stood before a large hump-shaped rock which sat in the middle of the trail. James didn't think it looked at all like a turtle.

"Why are we here?" he asked.

"Look!" Shanda led him around the back side of the boulder. There, slightly above eye level, a heart had been scratched in the surface of the rock. There were letters and words written inside, like a primitive valentine carved in stone.

James read: "Charlotte Bishop, the flower of the Mammoth Cave."

"Whoa," he whispered, "Did Stephen really write that?"

"Yes, he did. He loved his wife very much." Matthew spoke in hushed tones. James felt like they were in somewhere special, like a church or a library.

"What's amazing, among other things, is the handwriting," Matthew continued. "Do you two remember seeing Stephen's name in Gothic Avenue last night?"

"That's right!" Shanda spoke excitedly. "The names were badly printed, like a little kid was trying to write. These are beautiful."

"Very good, Shanda," Matthew said approvingly." Stephen actually learned to write by helping wealthy visitors make letters on the cave walls. His early examples are not at all neat. Eventually he became very good at it. This is one of his better samples."

As he spoke, Matthew unfolded a tripod and mounted a

camera on it. When he was all ready, he took half a dozen pictures of the inscription, with and without flash. "We'll see if any of those turn out decently," he commented. "I'd like to add them to my collection."

James felt a sense of awe at seeing this link to the past before him. "Thanks for letting me come with you, Matthew." He spoke in soft tones. "This is really amazing."

"It's my pleasure, son. This is Shanda's first visit here too."

They turned to leave Pensico Avenue, and Shanda spoke to her uncle. "We haven't shown James Stephen's map yet, Uncle Matthew."

"Well, that's true," Matthew agreed. "Let's see if we can take care of that next."

Heading back out the way they'd come, the small party came across a group of five or six bats flying through the cave. "That's good to see," said Matthew. "Their numbers seem to be increasing again."

"What do you mean, Uncle Matthew?" Shanda inquired. "Did there used to be more bats once?"

"Absolutely. In fact, Mammoth Cave once held the largest bat colony in the whole world. There were millions. But the natural entrance was blocked up for many years, and then the new entrance was too windy for them. Bats are particular in their hibernating needs. They won't just take a nap any old place."

"How many bats do you think are in this cave?" James asked.

"We think there may be five or ten thousand. It's not easy counting them; they move around a lot and live inside and outside the cave."

"Uncle Matthew, why do we usually only see one or two? Seems like they should be everywhere."

"Well, Shanda, it's like this. How would you feel if I brought a hundred people through your bedroom every hour and turned the lights on while you were trying to sleep?" Matthew smiled at the image.

James was trying to figure out how many tourists he could fit in his room. *"And here, ladies and gentlemen, the genius of Ohio. Please don't get loud, he's trying to sleep."*

"Anyway," Matthew continued, "our conservationists have been trying to recreate the original conditions to attract bats into the cave. They keep an eye on things like air flow and temperature. Like I said, it seems to be working."

They had reached the mouth of the cave and began walking up the hill back to the Visitors Center. It was already after noon, and James was starting to get hungry. He wanted to stay with his friends, but he knew better than to ask them to buy him lunch.

As usual, Matthew was ready for him. "How would you kids like to grab a sandwich at the coffee shop? My treat. After that maybe we can explore the world of Stephen Bishop."

"Thanks!" Both kids spoke at almost the same time. Apparently, James wasn't the only hungry one in the crowd.

"They have great BLT's, James," Shanda exclaimed. And for at least the tenth time in less than two days, James wondered why everyone in his hometown couldn't be this friendly.

Chapter VII

Shanda was right, of course. The BLT's were the best James had ever tasted. He felt proud to eat at the outdoor table with a park ranger. He could just imagine the visitors thinking: *That kid must be someone important. Not everyone gets to eat with the rangers.*

After a relaxing lunch break, the three friends returned to Matthew's office in the Visitors Center. Shanda picked up the story line. "The man who brought Stephen here was Franklin Gorin, who bought the cave in 1838. He paid five thousand dollars, which was a huge amount of money."

"I'll say," added James, "it would take me forever to get that kind of money."

"James!' Shanda sounded impatient. "Five thousand dollars

in those days would be millions today! Gorin was a really rich man."

"Anyway, Gorin sold the cave in late 1839 to a doctor from Louisville, a man named John Croghan. He's the one who set up the hospital we saw on Uncle Matthew's tour last night. He's also the one who got Stephen to make a map of the cave in 1842. Stephen made the map from memory, and it's still considered accurate today."

"Boy, Stephen Bishop must have been really something!" James blurted.

Shanda stopped talking and looked him in the eye. "That's what I've been telling you, James. The man was incredible. He even taught himself to read and write."

During their conversation, Matthew had been unlocking a metal cabinet at the back of the research office. "James, I can't let you touch this. This is a valuable historical artifact and we really don't want anything to happen to it."

Matthew produced a large tube. It looked like the inside tube of a roll of paper towels, except that it was twice that big and made out of heavy, black cardboard. He removed one end and carefully tapped on the other end, until a piece of paper slid out onto the desk. Using the eraser end of a pencil, Matthew carefully spread out the map's corners and weighted them down with small metal washers. James noticed that Matthew had put thin white gloves on his hands. "We don't ever handle this," he explained. "Our hands have a small amount of oil on them, which could ruin this map."

James thought that it was probably the coolest thing he'd ever seen. The map itself was on a yellowing paper, about the size of two notebook pages. The lines, which Stephen Bishop himself had drawn in 1842, were dark and clear. Cave passages were shown to be different sizes, corresponding to the sizes of the real openings. The map was thoroughly labeled, showing the underground maze leading away from the natural entrance to Mammoth Cave.

The three friends stared quietly at the map for several minutes. Finally, Shanda broke the silence. "Amazing, huh?"

James could only nod his head in agreement. There was something so powerful about this wonderful old map that he could barely speak. These lines, these very accurate drawings, were created by a young slave over a hundred and sixty years ago!

Ranger Matthew pointed out some areas of the cave which the kids knew already. "Here's the Star Chamber, where we were last night. Look, here's Gothic Avenue and the Rotunda. Over here is Pensico Avenue where we went this morning. Turtle Rock is probably about here." He pointed to a small lump in the trail.

"What is that small writing?" wondered James.

"I'm not sure what that says," Matthew answered. "There are several places on the map where Stephen made notes, but they're just about impossible to read. Here, take a look." He handed James a large magnifying glass. As the boy scanned the map, he saw many small notes on the edges and beside certain passages.

"The note next to Turtle Rock appears to say 'four feet left.' What's that for?"

He gave Shanda the magnifying glass.

"I can see that, too!" She was excited. "Uncle Matthew, have you noticed that before?"

"Not that particular note," Matthew replied. "I wouldn't get too excited about it, though. Stephen left a lot of notes about new passages to explore and about corrections he had to make."

James looked at Shanda to see what she was thinking, but her face gave no clue. She was intently studying the map.

After another ten minutes of studying the famous map, Matthew carefully rolled it up and put it back in the tube. "James, we'd best be getting you back to your family. If you've seen enough for one day, we'll run you home."

"It's been the best day I've had in a long time, Ranger Matthew. Thanks for taking me along and showing me the map."

"My pleasure, son. I'm glad to have some good company for Shanda, too. I'm afraid she's getting bored with no one but old people to talk to." Matthew had a slight smile on his face, as if he knew what was coming.

"No way, Uncle Matthew! I love being here with you guys! Anyway, you're not that old. I'm sure your Aunt Harriet would consider you a young man." Shanda smirked as she said this.

"What Aunt Harriet? I don't have an Aunt Harriet, and you know it."

"Oh, I thought you said Harriet Tubman was your aunt!" Shanda laughed out loud at her own joke, and she squealed as her uncle made a quick grab at her. Shanda was too quick for him, dancing out of his way easily. "My mistake, she was your sister!!"

Shanda was laughing uncontrollably now, and James and Matthew couldn't help but join in. "Panda Bear, you're in deep trouble next time I get hold of you!"

"You have to catch me first!" she cackled, dancing in front of her uncle, just out of reach.

Shanda's laughter, the beautiful Kentucky summer day, and the morning's caving adventure were almost too much for James. He felt so good he wanted to jump up and let out an Indian whoop.

As they the left the research office, James could tell something unusual was going on in the Visitors Center. Six rangers were walking by in a hurry, each equipped with a headlamp on a helmet. Their expressions were determined, as if they had something important on their minds. A young woman in coveralls appeared to be in charge of the group. Her name tag identified her as Ranger Patricia.

"Matthew, we need a hand." She spoke without stopping on her way toward the door. "Two teenage boys are lost in the cave!"

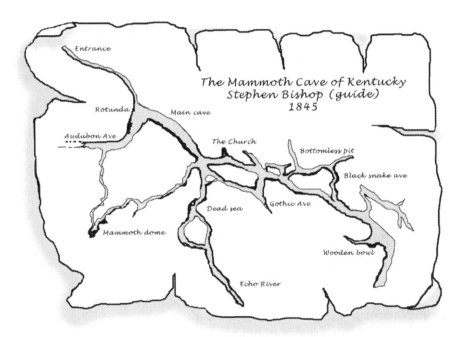

Chapter VIII

Immediately, all of their plans changed.

"James, can you call your mom to come pick you up?" Matthew asked. "I need to join the search party as soon as I can."

"Uncle Matthew," Shanda piped up. "Can James and I help with the search?"

"No, I'm afraid not. Our rangers have been trained for this emergency, and I'm afraid you'd only get in the way."

"But I know my way around the cave, and…"

"No!" Matthew was agitated, and clearly he was in no mood for games. "I said no, and I mean it. You'll have to find some other way to occupy yourself until we get these boys safely out of there. James, please use the phone in my office to call your parents."

As Matthew joined the other rangers in getting his spare lights and some water, the two new friends headed to his office.

Once inside, Shanda spoke up. "James, we can't just sit here and *do nothing*! Those boys need our help, and together we may be able to find them."

James couldn't believe what he was hearing! "Shanda, Matthew told you very clearly that you couldn't go with him. It would be dangerous and we'd be in the way."

"That's right, he said we couldn't go with him. But he never said we couldn't go on our own!"

"Shanda, that's crazy! We don't…

"James!" Shanda interrupted him. He had never seen her get excited in the short time since they'd met. "This not a game, it's a real life emergency! Those boys are lost. Imagine, if you and I walked out of the cave with those two. We'd be heroes! We'd be on TV, maybe on Oprah!!"

James could picture the famous TV star. *Next we have the two brave youngsters who saved the boys who were lost in Mammoth Cave. Please welcome James and Shanda!*

Shanda's excitement was getting infectious. Against his better judgment, James knew he was going to join her. "What if we get lost?" he protested. "How are we going to get into the cave with the door locked? Shanda, I don't even have a flashlight!"

"Where there's a will there's a way, James, and we have the will!" Shanda proclaimed. "PLEASE come with me. I can't go alone, you know that." She started rummaging around in Matthew's office. "Here, I've got a pack with a good cave map, and I can get us some helmets from the shelf. We'll need extra batteries for our head lamps. Get some bottles of water and some snack bars, would you?"

Having made up his mind to join her, James jumped into action. He had a thousand questions in his mind. "How often do people get lost in Mammoth Cave? Will they call the FBI? What about the people who are on tours in the cave?"

Shanda paid slight attention to him as she checked the helmet lights and made sure she had the right map. She opened the door to Matthew's office and looked out carefully. "Let's get out of here without being noticed," she suggested quietly.

They slipped out of the office door and then out of the Visitors Center without attracting any attention. Outside, it was still a beautiful summer day. Park visitors were chatting and laughing in the warm sunshine. A group of tourists were busy posing for pictures, jabbering away in some language he'd never heard before.

"Shanda," he asked as they walked past the group, "what language were those Chinese people talking in?"

Shanda snorted loudly, as if she were trying to cut off a laugh. "I'm guessing it would be Chinese, James." She smiled her devious grin at him, just to let him know that he'd asked another ridiculous question.

James didn't mind; he and Shanda were already good enough friends that he could stand a little teasing. Shanda spoke up again, "People very rarely get lost in the cave. You noticed last night how careful Uncle Matthew and Kasey were to keep track of everyone. Once every five or six years, some tourist thinks it's OK to wander away from the group down one of the side passages. What they don't realize is that the trailing ranger on each trip is turning the lights out behind each group. Once that happens, they're stuck in the dark until help comes."

James shivered. He didn't want to imagine being stuck alone in the dark in a huge cave. He remembered the story of Tom Sawyer and Becky Thatcher, and how they'd almost given up hope of getting out alive.

"I've never heard of the park service calling for extra help. The law enforcement rangers here are unbelievable, the best in the country. And sure, the tours keep going. There are a lot of people visiting, and there's no need to get everyone in a panic."

They were walking quickly down the hill to the cave entrance as they talked. Halfway down, they passed a young ranger giving his safety talk before taking a group into the cave. "Please don't take flash pictures of bats. Their eyes are extremely sensitive to light."

At the entrance, James saw another ranger standing at the top of the stairs leading down into the cave. "Hi Shanda," he greeted the girl. "Who's your new friend?"

"Ranger Wendell, this is James. He's from Ohio. Ranger Courtney is his aunt, and they're visiting for a whole week!"

"Well, that's great!" Ranger Wendell exclaimed, smiling a big smile at the kids. "We sure are happy to have you here at Mammoth Cave, young man." James had a great feeling, like they'd just shared some very funny joke together. *Another nice person*, he thought to himself. *Maybe I can talk Mom and Dad into moving to Kentucky.*

"Ranger Wendell, is the self-guided tour open? I'd like to show James the Rotunda."

"Well, Shanda, we'll keep it open until about three o'clock today. Of course you can take a look around. Tell your Uncle Matthew I'll put two tickets on his credit card."

The kids laughed at his joke and thanked him for letting them go have a look. They headed down the stairs into the big cave entrance.

James couldn't believe it. They were heading into Mammoth Cave on their own!

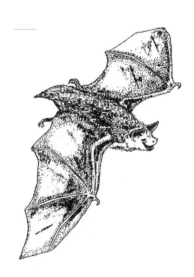

Chapter IX

Shanda led the way into the Rotunda, the large room they had visited the night before. People taking the self-guided Discovery Tour were walking around the room, taking pictures and chatting with the ranger on duty. She was explaining to a group of German tourists about the significance of the saltpeter mining operation before them.

"Hi Judy," James heard Shanda speak in the shadows.

Range Judy turned. "Oh, hi Shanda. I didn't see you come in. What are you up to today?"

"This is my new friend James. I thought I'd show him the old mine sites."

"Pleased to meet you James." Judy smiled. She turned away as a family with four kids entered the large cave room. "Good afternoon, folks. Welcome to Mammoth Cave. We have some bats sleeping on the ceiling today. Would you like to see them?"

Shanda took her opportunity while Judy was distracted. "Ranger Judy," she said, "I'm going to show James the other mine site. We'll be right back." Without waiting to see if the ranger had heard her, she tugged James by the arm, pulling him toward the large passage known as Broadway.

"Where are we going?" James whispered. He was nervous, but he didn't want to give away Shanda's plan at this point.

"Relax," she replied. "I know the rangers here, so they let me get away with small favors from time to time. You just have to know how to play the game." James recalled having the same thought himself, not that long ago in Ms. Wilson's class. Here in the huge cave passages with his new friend, school seemed a million miles away.

Without looking back, Shanda took them under the rope at the edge of the self-guided route. They headed down the large passage leading out of the Rotunda. James kept expecting Ranger Judy to call them back or stop them, but they walked further and further up the boardwalk without interruption.

"This is where we came last night," James said aloud, as he realized where they were.

"Yes it is, and it's where we started out toward Turtle Rock this morning," Shanda added. "In fact, that's where I want to look first."

In his nervousness at getting by the rangers, James had completely forgotten about the lost boys. Suddenly the huge size of Mammoth Cave became very apparent to him. "Do you really think we'll find them?" he asked.

"I don't know James, but we wouldn't feel right if we didn't try. Besides, there's something else I want to take a look at."

That last statement caught James off guard. "Shanda, we came in here to help the search party, right? I mean, you're not taking me somewhere where we shouldn't go, are you?"

Shanda laughed her nice easy laugh. "Relax, James. As soon as we lifted that rope and went under it, we went somewhere we shouldn't have. But no, I'm not taking you anywhere dangerous. Let's put our helmets on."

The young cavers had rounded the first corner in the mammoth passage, leaving them in near darkness. They opened up the pack and put on their caving helmets. Switching on their head lamps, they were rewarded with the comforting bright beams. For the second time in just a few hours, James and Shanda were exploring Mammoth Cave without the electric lights on. But this time, they were alone!

At first, both the explorers were nervous. They knew they should never be doing this alone, and they also knew they could get into big trouble for doing it. But sometimes young people will encourage each other in doing something they want to do, even if they know it might not be a good idea. Deep down, they both wanted to explore a bit of cave without an adult there to watch them.

Shanda set a brisk pace down Broadway. She and James talked in quiet tones as they walked by the second saltpeter mine, past Booth's amphitheater, then Standing Rock, and over a small hill to the Giant's Coffin. Striding through the darkness alone, the cave's magic was complete. James felt a heightened sense of every shadow, every sharp rock. He and Shanda were true explorers, pushing deeper into the vast darkness.

They didn't meet a soul as they walked, which was fine with them. They really didn't want to have to answer any questions about what they were doing in the cave alone. Ten minutes later they were back in Pensico Avenue, heading toward Turtle Rock.

At the rock, Shanda turned to face James. In the darkness of the cave, she had an otherworldly look that he found fascinating. "James, I need to tell you something now."

Her voice sounded strained, which made the boy pay more attention than usual. Shanda was clearly excited.

"I've got a secret I've never shared with anyone, James. I think I know the secret to Mammoth Cave."

"What...?" James didn't finish his sentence, as the truth dawned on him. He stammered "Do you mean...?"

"Yes, James. I know where Stephen hid his treasure!"

As soon as she'd spoken the words, James realized that Shanda had intended to come here all along!

"You never meant to come look for those boys, did you?" He sounded distressed. "It was all just an excuse to come back to Turtle Rock alone!"

"I'm sorry I tricked you James, but I've been waiting a long time for the chance to get in the cave by myself. And besides, I needed you. I know better than to come in here alone." Shanda looked serious, and James thought she really did feel a little guilty about tricking him.

"Anyway," she continued. "Would you have come with me if I'd told you the truth?"

Probably not, thought James. "OK, we're here, let's make the most of it. Tell me the rest of your secret. What makes you think Stephen's metal box is near here?"

"Because of his map, James. Right near here, the note said "four feet left." Uncle Matthew thought he might be referring to a side passage, but I don't think so. Do you see any side passage around here?"

Both of them looked with their head lamps, sweeping their helmets slowly side to side. There were no other passages at all, just the one they were standing in. And right in the middle of Pensico Avenue stood Turtle Rock.

"So what do you think his note means? Is there something four feet to the left of this rock?" James was getting as excited as Shanda. He walked to the edge of the rock as he spoke, pacing off four steps from one end. The trail looked hard-packed in all directions.

"This used to be a tourist trail, back in the old days." Shanda informed him. "Many thousands of people have walked here since Stephen stood here. If there were something under this trail that he had buried in the 1840's, it would be impossible to tell that today. Besides, there's another problem. The left side of the rock depends on which way you're facing it. If we'd been coming the other way, then "four feet left" would mean we'd have to look on the other side of this passage."

James could see her point, but he felt confused. Even if Shanda was right about the note on the map, they didn't seem to be any closer to locating Stephen Bishop's mystery box. "What do you think?" he asked. "What does the note mean?"

Shanda looked thoughtful. "We know that Charlotte was the dearest person in the world to Stephen." She said slowly. "And right here, on Turtle Rock, is the famous heart he scratched." They walked over to the heart they'd seen and photographed with Matthew earlier in the day.

Charlotte Bishop, the flower of the Mammoth Cave. The two friends stood transfixed, thinking about the young slave who had scratched the message to his beloved wife so many years ago. "James," Shanda spoke in a whisper. "The treasure is four feet to the left of this heart!"

As soon as she had spoken these words, James knew with all his heart that she was right. He only wished he'd thought of it first.

Together, they pointed their lamps at the ground, four feet left of a spot below the heart. At first they saw nothing. Then James spoke up. "Look at that smaller rock! It looks like it's been placed right against the base of the boulder!"

Immediately, they dropped to their knees and started digging with their hands. They scraped dirt around from the base of the smaller rock, trying to make handholds they could use to lift it. As they dug, they exposed more and more of the rock to view. After just a few minutes of digging, they were ready.

"Let's slow down one minute." Shanda spoke up. "If Stephen's treasure really is here, we're about to make history. We may be about to solve the mystery of Mammoth Cave. It's baffled everyone for over one hundred sixty years."

As James looked as Shanda, he saw that she was beaming with anticipation. He knew he was grinning from ear to ear. His heart was thumping like it would jump out of his chest. "OK, on three." He said. "One, two, three!"

They put their hands under the edges of the rock and lifted with all their might. The rock shifted, then came up in their hands. Underneath was a small, red, metal box!

Chapter X

Things happened in a blur after that. Both of them stood in dumbfounded amazement, not sure what to do next.

"James, we've got to take this to Uncle Matthew," Shanda said at last. They both knew they would get into trouble for coming into the cave alone, but right at this moment, they didn't care. "Can you hold the rock up by yourself?" she asked.

"Sure," James assured her. He wasn't at all sure he could do it, but now wasn't the time to admit something like that.

Shanda slowly loosened her grip, and James strained to hold up the edge of the limestone slab. Quickly, Shanda's hand shot underneath and retrieved the box. It was about eight inches long and maybe six inches wide. Once she got her hands safely out of the way, James let the rock crash back into place.

Neither of them wanted to open the box. It seemed too important. They turned it over carefully, examining all sides. It appeared to be well-used, and it looked as if it had been banged up by repeated dropping. There were many small dents in its top and sides. After checking it out for a few minutes, the two friends finally relaxed and smiled at each other. They were both nervous, and they were both very happy. They had found Stephen Bishop's lost treasure! They began to make their way back out of the cave.

The next morning James and Shanda were sitting in a conference room, along with James's parents, Ranger Matthew, and a number of other adults in park uniforms. The two kids had explained everything to their family members the evening before, confessing all that they had done to go into the cave alone. They had handed the red metal box to Matthew, who seemed deeply moved to receive the treasure.

James's parents had been very unhappy with him. "James, we trusted you," his dad had told him. "If you want more freedom and more responsibility in your life, you have to prove to us you can make good decisions. When you lose someone's trust, you've lost something that's very hard to get back."

James knew what his parents had said was true. He had known they shouldn't have gone into the cave alone, even as they were walking down the stairs into the entrance.

"Well, let's begin." A voice at the end of the table snapped him back to the meeting room. "Mr. and Mrs. Murphy, my name is Mr. Thompson. I'm the superintendent here at the park. You've met Matthew, of course, and these other folks are Joyce, Charles, and Rob. There are many people in the park who would love to be in this room with us, but these three are our best historians and biographers of Stephen."

James wondered how it could be that Stephen Bishop was so famous that he didn't even need his last name to be recognized. Everyone simply knew who Stephen was. Just like Elvis, or Cleopatra. His mind wandered: *Folks, this could be James's greatest discovery.* Shanda noticed he was daydreaming and kicked his ankle under the table.

"Before we continue, I need to speak directly to James and Shanda for a minute. I know you two kids meant well, but your behavior last night was inexcusable. You should *never* have entered the cave on your own, and I believe you knew that when you did. You put yourselves in a potentially dangerous situation, and I am relieved that no harm came to you. By the way, the two boys whom we were looking for turned up about the time you were finding this box. They are safely back with their families.

As to the box, we have another problem. It's important for archaeologists to study artifacts where they are found, so they can understand the circumstances at the time they were left. By removing this box from the cave, you have done us a great disservice. Our scientists can never study it in an undisturbed condition."

James and Shanda began to realize how foolish they had been. They had been way too excited to consider the consequences of their actions when they removed the box from the cave.

Mr. Thompson continued. "The circumstances of your finding this box, if true, are certainly remarkable. How it could have lain there for a hundred and sixty years unnoticed by all those cavers is beyond me. Before I open this, I need to warn everyone here. We don't know if what this contains is of any historical value or if it's even genuine. We have to consider the possibility that we're dealing with a hoax here."

"No sir! This is NOT a hoax!" Shanda interrupted quickly. "James and I found that box using Stephen's map, just like we told you."

The superintendent smiled. "I'm sure you did, Shanda. We're just not sure yet who put the box under that rock. That's all I'm saying. I don't want to get our hopes up too high just yet."

Then open the darn box, already! James thought. *Enough of this talk, talk, talk.*

As if he had heard him, Mr. Thompson began to tap on the edges of the box with a small screwdriver. After loosening any grit he could see, he carefully began to pry off the lid.

James and Shanda were beside themselves with excitement. What could be in such a small box that would have made Stephen a rich man? And where did it come from? Everyone in the room leaned forward in anticipation as the lid came off with a small pop.

Inside the box was a single piece of paper, which was folded in half. Ranger Matthew offered his tweezers and weights to Mr. Thompson, who spread the document on the table.

The park historians studied the page for a minute. Joyce reacted first. "Oh my goodness!" She was deeply moved, and she made no effort to conceal her emotions. Tears formed in her eyes.

Charles and Matthew were both breathing deeply, as if they were trying to keep their composure. *Whatever this is,* thought James, *it sure has their attention.* He and his parents and Shanda waited for the others to collect themselves and tell them what was going on.

After another few minutes, the superintendent began to read. He was overcome with emotion, and he occasionally had to stop reading and breathe deeply.

To whom it may concern, the paper began, *I, Dr. John Croghan, being of sound mind and body, do, on this First Day of January, in the year 1849, make the following amendments to my will.*

"He was the owner of Mammoth Cave, as well as Stephen's owner at that time," Joyce explained to the visitors. "As a matter of fact, he died in 1849 from consumption."

The superintendent continued.

Most of those reading this document will know that I made the purchase of the great Mammoth Cave of Kentucky in 1839. I was interested in developing this wonder for more visitors to come and see, and I was equally committed to finding a cure for consumption. That dreaded disease has taken my own brother, and I fear from my symptoms that I may be the next to succumb to its ravages.

"Croghan knew he was going to die!" Charles interjected. "He made this last amendment to his will to try to set things right."

Also in 1839, the document continued, *I met a young boy named Stephen Bishop. This remarkable young man has done more to unfold the mysteries of my beautiful cave than any other human alive. He has explored and mapped many miles of this subterranean giant, entirely for the joy of the discovery. The credit for all my financial success in this area lies at the feet of the great Stephen.*

As I have never had a child of my own, I have come to think of Stephen as one of my own. For those of you who think it irregular that I should become attached to a slave, rest assured that I am entirely serious in this matter. He is as family to me.

Because of the difference in our stations, I have remained aloof from him these many years. But now, I wish to amend this last will and testament in his favor.

The group sat in stunned silence as they saw what was unfolding. Dr. John Croghan, the famous Louisville doctor and owner of Mammoth Cave, had included Stephen in his will. The park historians looked at each other, as they began to understand the full importance of the revelation.

"Croghan never had any children." Joyce said. "And in 1849, a slave would have had no chance of being recognized as being his legal heir. In today's terms, the good doctor would have been a multimillionaire."

Ranger Matthew spoke. "Is there more?"

"Yes, there is." Mr. Thompson continued reading.

As the fear of death hangs over me, I have decided to take an action I should have taken decades ago. I am proud to acknowledge Stephen as my heir and to amend my will accordingly. Therefore, upon my death, I leave all my property in Edmonson County, Kentucky, including the great Mammoth Cave, to Stephen Bishop.

The superintendent's hands shook slightly as he read, and his voice cracked with emotion.

This document is in direct opposition to my former will and testament. This paper, signed by me on January 1st, 1849, replaces all former documents and renders them invalid. It is my expressed intention that my slave, Stephen Bishop, shall inherit the entirety of Mammoth Cave.

Everyone was stunned.

"Can this possibly be real?" whispered Charles.

"It appears to be so." Rob had been studying the page carefully. "The will is dated, signed and witnessed. Dr. Croghan even had his attorney attach his seal to the bottom of the page."

"Mammoth Cave belonged to Stephen!" Shanda screamed. She jumped up, unable to contain herself. "Uncle Matthew! James! Stephen owned the cave that he loved so much!"

Her irrepressible energy was contagious. In the flash of an eye, the entire mood of the group changed. They each knew the importance of their discovery, and they were all thrilled to be the first ones to see it.

James's mom had a question. "Stephen never established his claim to the cave. Why didn't he produce this document when Dr. Croghan died?"

They all considered this for a minute.

Charles spoke up first. "He may have thought that Croghan's original heirs would fight it in court. They could have afforded good lawyers, and they all had plenty to lose if Stephen did inherit the cave. It was a real moneymaker by then."

Joyce added her thoughts. "That's probably right. Even with this paper in his hand, Stephen probably realized he would never get a court to recognize him as the owner of Mammoth Cave in those days. After all, he was still a slave at the time of the doctor's death." The group nodded in agreement.

"I'm not so sure about all that." Ranger Matthew had been listening to the conversation, and now he spoke up. "You're probably right about Stephen's chances of actually getting ownership of the cave, but I don't think that was the reason he left this paper buried. He had come to this place as a teenage boy, and over the next ten years had become a very successful cave explorer, guide, and mapmaker. He was famous. He had a wife and a son whom he loved dearly. Also, Dr. Croghan's first will had granted him his freedom. I think he made a choice between the life he knew and loved and a life he felt unprepared for. How could a slave take over ownership of an inn and a tour business? He would have become rich, but at what cost to himself and his family? I think he just decided to pass up the money and keep his happiness."

Heads nodded, and the adults smiled knowingly. Everyone was exhausted; it had been an emotional meeting. They had solved the mystery of Mammoth Cave, or most of it anyway.

"Shanda and James," superintendent Thompson spoke. "You have made a discovery of tremendous importance to the National Park Service and to the United States. I will recommend you for park service awards, which you richly deserve." His eyes shone with pride, and the two kids felt both pleased and awkward to be congratulated in front of the group.

"Uncle Matthew," Shanda was whispering, but everyone could still hear her. "Does this mean I'm not grounded from going in the cave after all?"

"Not on your life, young lady," Matthew laughed. "You knew that was wrong when you did it, so now you must accept the consequences. I am proud of you two, though." He wrapped his arms around the two kids in a big bear hug.

"Maybe you can spend some time at the zoo with your fat furry friends." James chimed in. "The pandas!" He laughed.

He wasn't quick enough to get out of the room before she tackled him and did a little enforcing of her own.

Last Will and Testament of Dr. John Croghan

Chapter XI

The vacation was almost over. As punishment for his disobedience, James had not been allowed to reenter the cave during the week. It pained him greatly, especially when teams of archaeologists and photographers returned to Turtle Rock. The investigation went on without him. News of their discovery had spread rapidly throughout the park service, and he and Shanda became instant celebrities with the park rangers.

James and his parents had spent a great week, though. They had hiked the hilly trails in the park and had taken an overnight canoe trip on the Green River. James had been pretty sure that he had spotted a black bear along the river bank. Ranger Matthew told him no one had seen a bear in over a century, but James wasn't so sure.

On their last night in the cabin, his mom told him they were going to a party. Without saying much more about it, they headed down the road toward Aunt Courtney and Uncle

Richard's place. When they arrived, James was amazed to see about twenty cars parked at various angles along the sides of their lane.

"Welcome, you buckeyes!" Richard hollered. "'Bout time you showed up. We couldn't eat without the guest of honor!"

James looked around at all the smiling faces. He recognized almost everyone. Park rangers and friends stood around, chatting and eyeing the grill. They all took turns congratulating him and telling him to come back soon.

Soon Aunt Courtney gave the signal, and the feast began. The crowd dug into massive platters of corn on the cob, fresh garden beans, salad, homemade bread of all types, and several other garden dishes which James didn't recognize. And, of course, Uncle Richard's famous barbecued chicken.

James hunted around the group until he found Shanda.

"Hey," he greeted her.

"Hey, yourself." Shanda smiled.

Without thinking much about it, James asked "Do you think you might come see us in Ohio sometime? I'd love to have you come visit."

"That would be way cool, James. The famous cave explorers' reunion!" she laughed. "Maybe I can get Uncle Matthew to take me up there before I have to go home."

The two friends chatted and laughed throughout the evening. James told her stories of all the times he'd been in trouble with Ms. Wilson and Mr. Curtis. Shanda had some pretty good tales to tell herself.

Finally, the evening was over and the partiers were leaving.

"I have something for you, James." Shanda said. "I went to the zoo." She opened her hand to reveal a small black and white pin.

"Thanks, Panda." said James. "This will remind me of you until next time I see you."

The next day, the Murphys were in the driveway bright and early.

"Your suitcase."

"Check."

"My suitcase."

"Check."

"Swimming gear and towels."

"Check."

"Food and snacks."

"Check"

"Fishing gear and tackle box."

"Check."

"Dad's girlie magazines."

"JAMES!"

The trip home went by quickly. They stopped for lunch just outside Cincinnati and made it home by midafternoon. The phone rang just as they entered the house.

James's mom picked it up. "Yes, this is the Murphys. Yes, he's here, just a minute please."

"Guess what, James?" She sounded excited. "It's someone from the Oprah show!"